Frank was a monster who wanted to dance.
So he put on his hat and his shoes made in France
and opened a jar and put **ants** in his pants.

So begins this monstrously funny, deliciously disgusting, horrifyingly hilarious story of a monster who follows his dream. Keith Graves' wacky illustrations and laugh-out-loud text will tickle the funny bone and leave readers clamoring for an encore.

2005 Book Sense Top Ten Pick for Halloween

"Just the ticket." —*Booklist*

"... [will] hit primary graders' funny bones." —*Publishers Weekly*

"Young listeners will respond to the comedy, the catchy rhythm, and especially the yuck factor." —*The Bulletin of the Center for Children's Books*

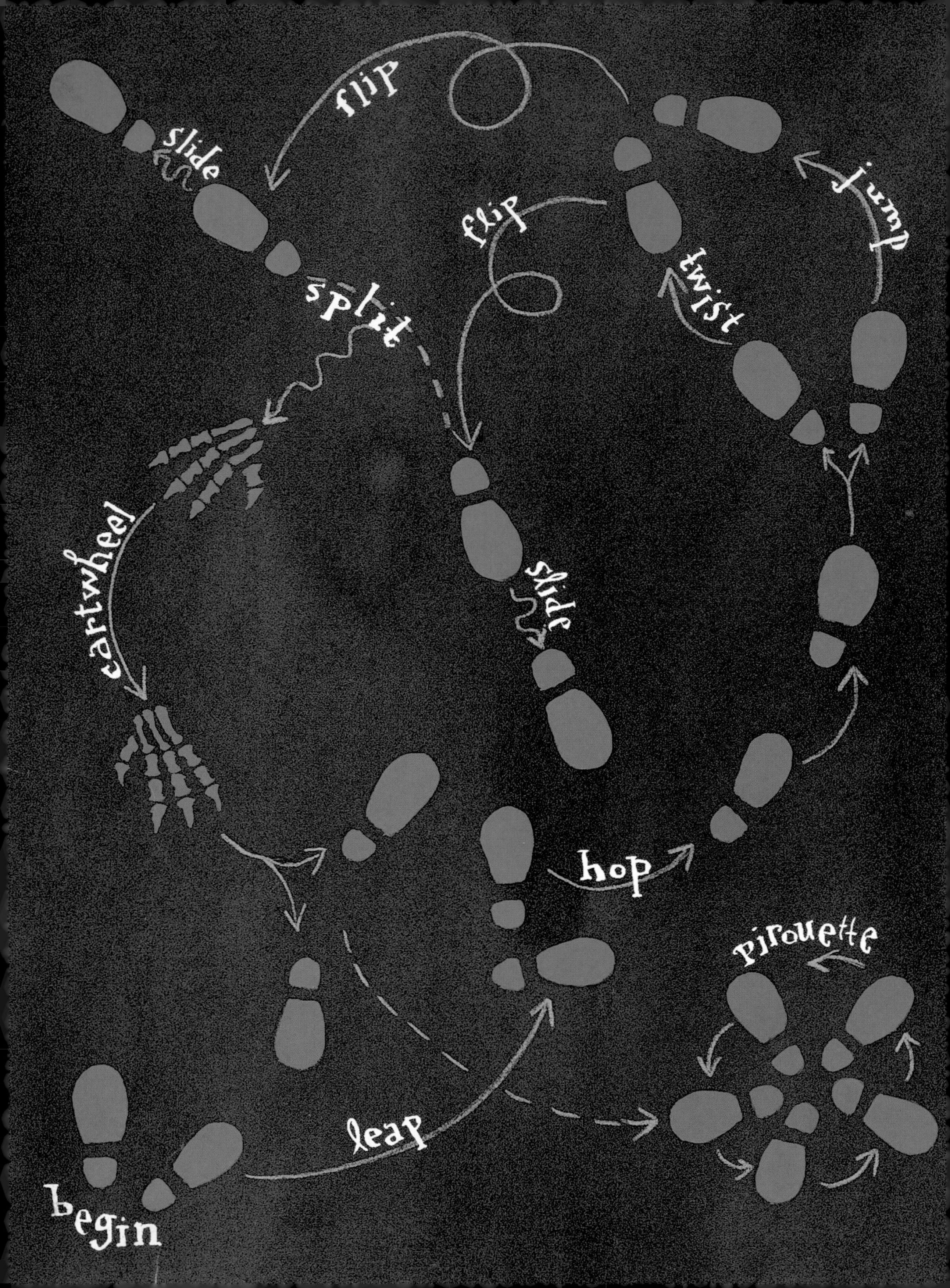
begin
leap
hop
slide
flip
split
cartwheel
slide
flip
twist
jump
pirouette

end

re-attach

leg in

mid-leap

end toss

hand-walk

detach leg

hop

hop

hop

bop

For Max and Emma, audacious dancers in their own right.

First paperback edition published in 2006 by Chronicle Books LLC.

Text and illustrations © 1999 by Keith Graves.

Book design by Susan Van Horn.
The illustrations in this book were rendered in acrylic paints and colored pencils.
Manufactured in China.
ISBN-10 0-8118-5452-3
ISBN-13 978-0-8118-5452-8

The Library of Congress has catalogued the previous edition as follows:

Graves, Keith.
Frank was a monster who wanted to dance / by Keith Graves.
p.   cm.
Summary: Frank the monster indulges his love of dancing by strutting
his stuff on stage until his head unzips, his brains flop out, and he
continues to lose body parts.
ISBN 0-8118-2169-2
[1. Monsters—Fiction. 2. Dance—Fiction. 3. Stories in rhyme.]
I. Title.
PZ8.3.G74243Fr   1999
[E]—dc21 98-36189
CIP
AC

Distributed in Canada by Raincoast Books
9050 Shaughnessy Street, Vancouver, British Columbia V6P 6E5

10 9 8 7 6 5 4 3 2 1

Chronicle Books LLC
85 Second Street, San Francisco, California 94105

www.chroniclekids.com

Frank was a MONSTER

who wanted to DANCE

by keith graves

chronicle books · san francisco

Frank was a monster who wanted to dance.

So he put on his hat and
his shoes made in France

and opened a jar
and put **ants** in his pants.

He drove to the theater

and jumped onstage.

Then he
danced
like his shoe size
instead of his age!

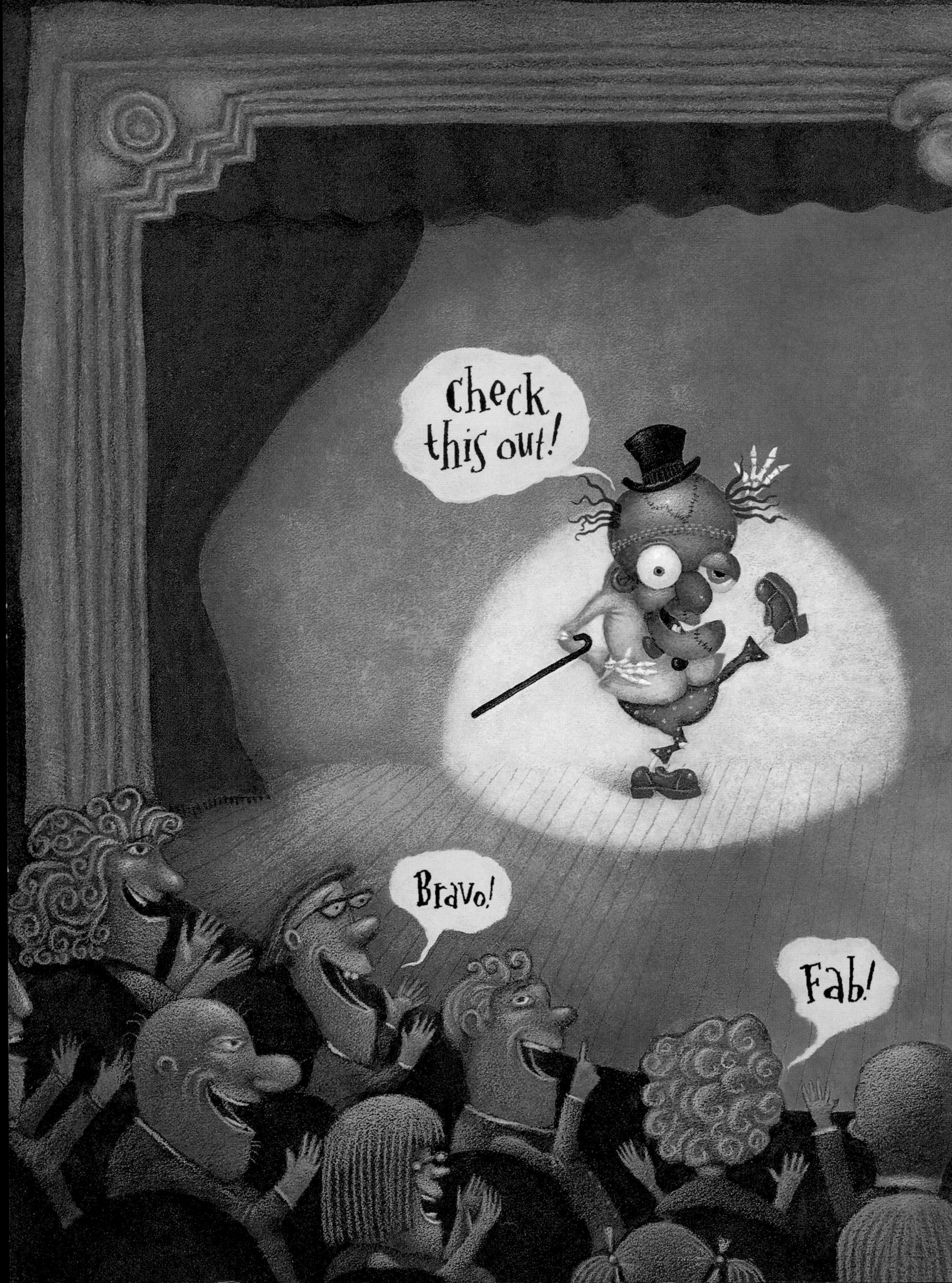
Check this out!
Bravo!
Fab!

Frank did a cartwheel!

Yippie!

Yow!

Frank did a flip.

Suddenly his head began to unZip.

OUT flopped his brain...

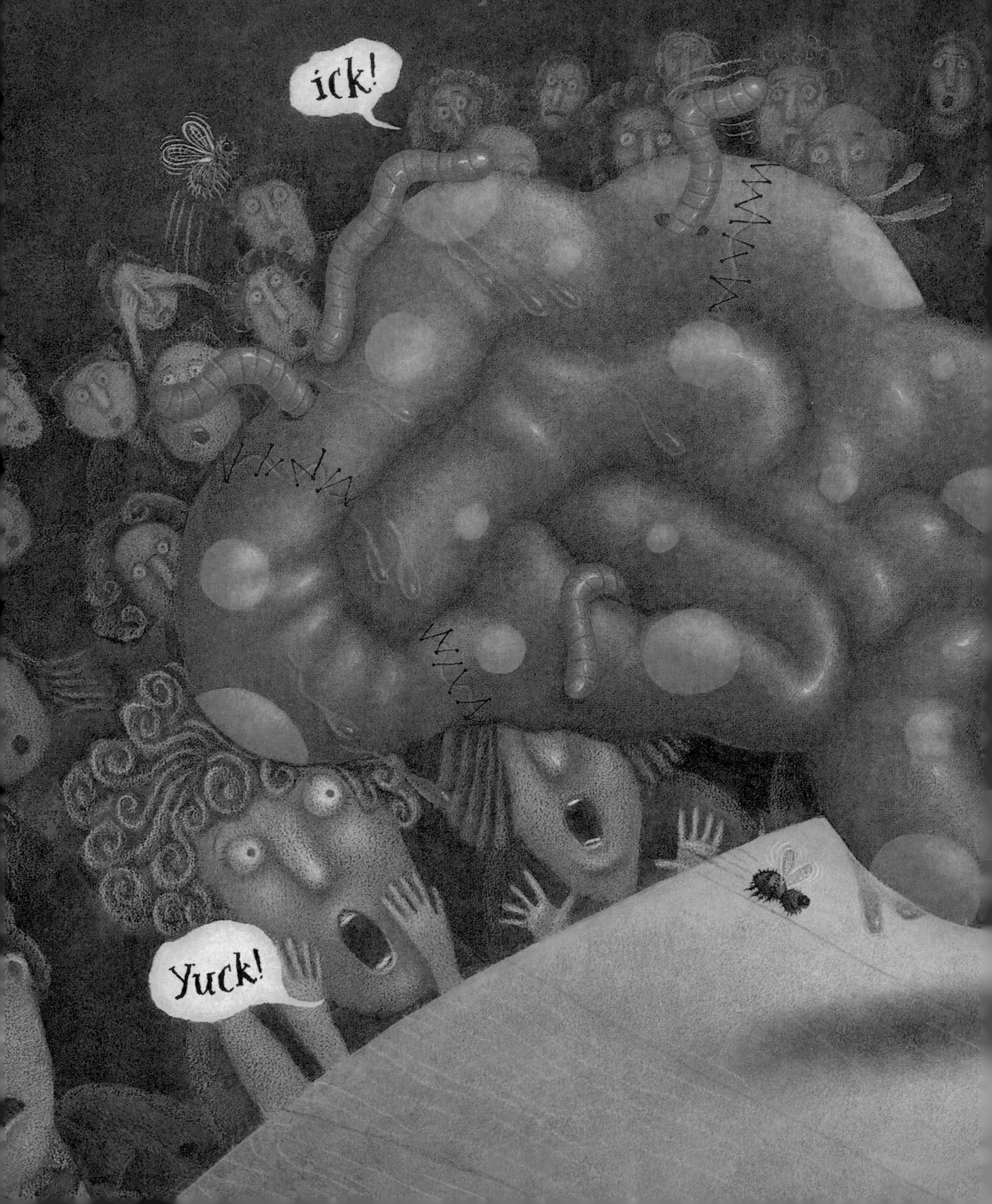

which loosened

his eyeball

which rolled out the door.

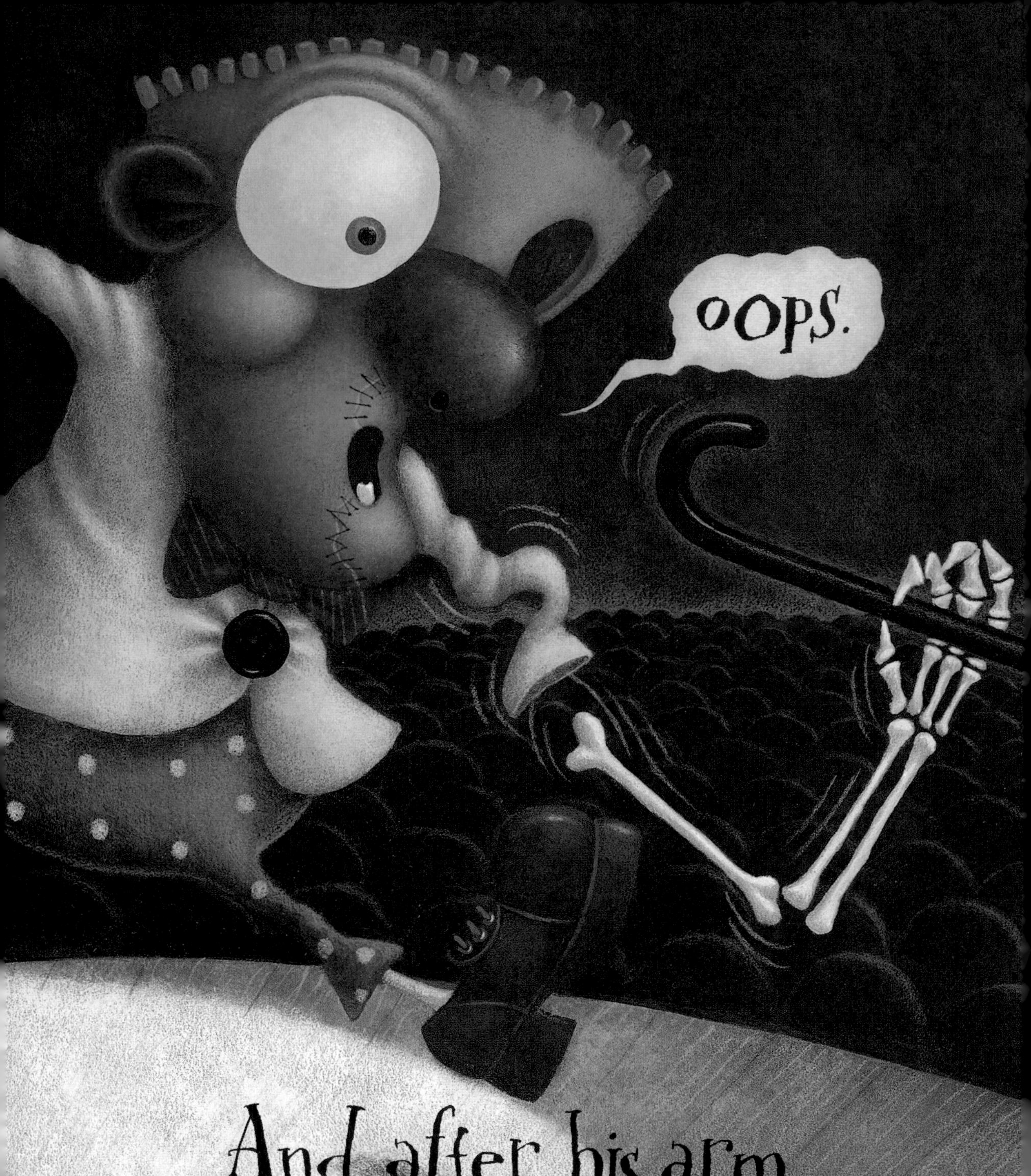

And after his arm
fell out of his sleeve,

the horrified audience started to leave.

But Frank kept dancing.
He said, *what the heck?*

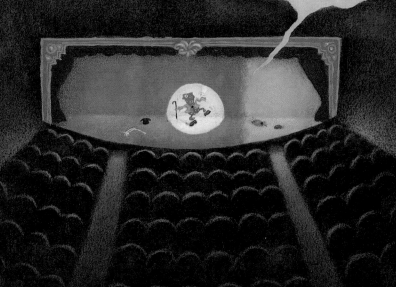

and laughed as his head
fell off of his neck.

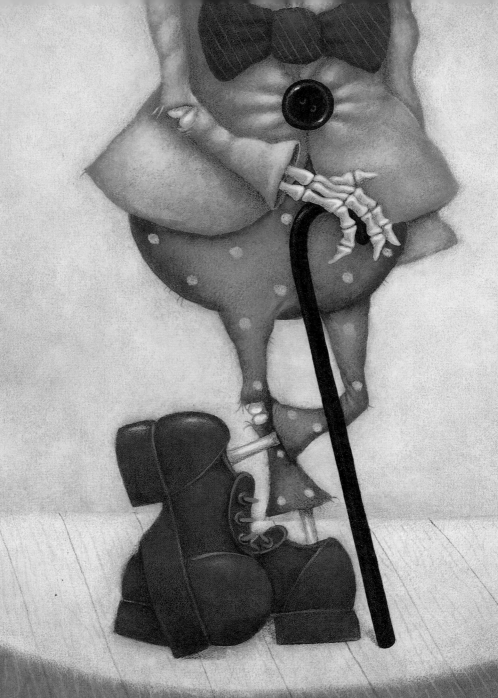

He said to himself
with a one-eyed glance,

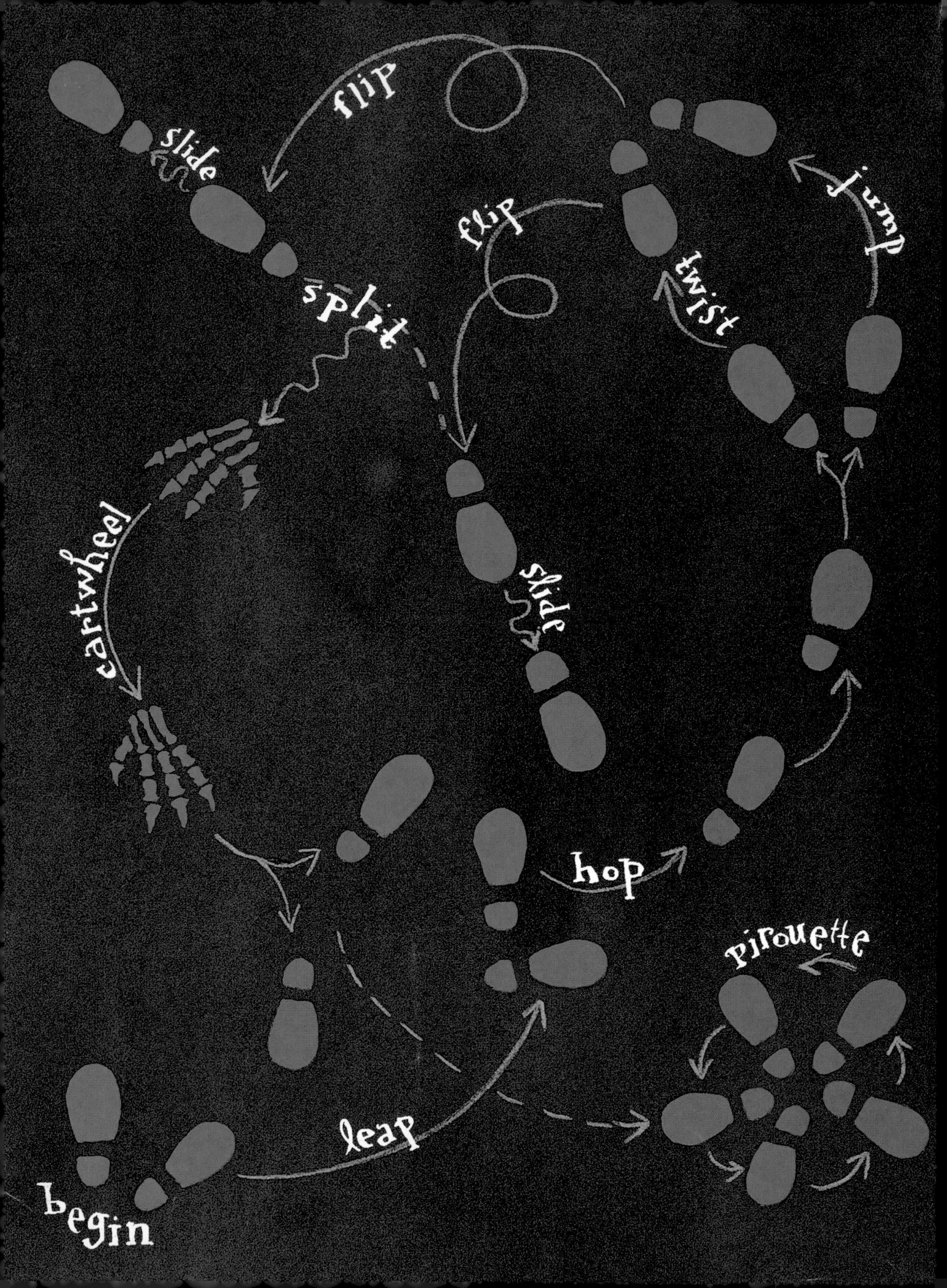

flip

slide

flip

jump

twist

split

cartwheel

slide

hop

pirouette

leap

begin

end

re-attach

leg in

mid-leap

hand-
walk

and loss

detach leg

hop

hop

hop

hop

 is a human who always wanted to be a monster, but never had the right shoes. He is the author-illustrator of several other books, including *Pet Boy*, which *Kirkus Reviews* described as "bursting with color and a host of strange creatures" and of which *Booklist* said, "delivers a worthy thought with engaging silliness." Keith lives somewhere in the middle of Texas with a lovely princess and little twin monsters.